THIS BOOK BELONGS TO:

_____

For Isla. S.D.
For Chris and Kai. C.C.

This paperback edition first published in 2014 by
Andersen Press Ltd.,
20 Vauxhall Bridge Road, London SW1V 2SA.
Published in Australia by Random House Australia Pty.,
Level 3, 100 Pacific Highway, North Sydney, NSW 2060.
First published in Great Britain in 2013
by Andersen Press Ltd.
Text copyright © Stephen Davies, 2013.
Illustration copyright © Christopher Corr, 2013.
The rights of Stephen Davies and Christopher Corr to be identified as
the author and illustrator of this work have been asserted by them
in accordance with the Copyright, Designs and Patents Act, 1988.
All rights reserved.
Colour separated in Switzerland by Photolitho AG, Zürich.
Printed and bound in Malaysia by Tien Wah Press.
10 9 8 7 6 5 4 3 2 1

British Library Cataloguing in Publication Data available.
ISBN 978 1 84939 5311

DON'T SPILL THE MILK!

Stephen Davies   Christopher Corr

ANDERSEN PRESS

Penda lived in a tiny village in Africa with her mum and her aunties. It was rainy season, so Penda's dad was up in the grasslands looking after the sheep.

"Penda," said her mum one day, "I'm going to take a bowl of
milk to Daddy. I will be back this afternoon."
"I know where the grasslands are," said Penda. "Let
me take Daddy his milk. Please, please, please!"

"All right," said her mum, "but try not to spill any milk on the way."
Penda ran to milk the cow.
She filled a bowl, put it on her head, stood up and began to walk.

Steady, Penda whispered to herself, gently does it, girl.
Don't wiggle, don't wobble, don't try to rush it, girl.

Penda picked a path across
the uppy, downy dunes,
past a caravan of camels and
a flock of desert jinns.

Don't slip, don't slide, girl, don't fall over.
Don't let a single droplet drop on the sand.

It was the day of the rainy season mask dance.
Penda wove her way amid a million dancing beasties.

Walk tall, walk steady,
eyes on the horizon, girl.
Don't even think about
spilling any milk.

The great River Niger
was dark and wide.

Penda took a ride in
a stinky fishing boat.

Don't shiver, don't quiver,
don't fall in the river, girl.

Keep it on your head,
girl, milk don't float.

Fifteen pale giraffes were stalking across the plains
like fifteen aliens on a dusty moon.

Don't look, don't turn your head,
just walk on through. You're not at the zoo,
girl, you've got work to do.

Oh no! One final mountain looming high!
Penda breathed in deep and up she climbed.

Left foot, right foot, never give up, girl.
Left hand, right hand, all the way up now.

At last Penda arrived
at the grasslands! A flock of woolly sheep
were munching grass, and there
in the middle, chilling in the shade
of a mango tree, sat Penda's dad.

"Hi, Daddy."
"Hi, Penda. Nice to see you."
"I've brought you some milk," said Penda.
She took the bowl off her head, but just
as she was passing it to **Daddy** . . .

SPLOSH!

A big fat mango landed
right in the bowl!
Daddy's milk spilt
everywhere.

"I don't believe it!" wailed Penda. "I carried that milk for miles and miles over the dunes and across the river and up the mountain and I didn't stop to watch the mask dance or the white giraffes, because I didn't want to spill a single drop and now look — IT'S ALL GONE!"

Daddy gave Penda a big hug.
"It's not all gone," he whispered. "There was more than milk in that bowl."
"Huh?" said Penda.

"It's true," said Daddy. "Your love for me was in that bowl as well.
You carried it over the dunes and across the river and up the mountain.
You carried it past the mask dance and the white giraffes.
You brought it all the way up to the grasslands and you gave it to me just fine.
That bowl was full of love, girl, and it still is. You didn't spill a drop."

Penda wiped away her tears.
She pointed at the big fat mango.
"I think it must be lunchtime,"
she said.

"I agree," said Daddy. "As it happens, I prefer mango to milk any day."
Daddy took a knife and cut the mango into three big, juicy pieces.

Penda ate that first piece.
"Yummy!" she said.
Daddy ate the second
piece. "Scrummy!" he said.

The third piece was still in
the bowl. "For Mummy?"
asked Penda.
"That's right," said Daddy.

"Tell her it comes with all my love!"

Also by Stephen Davies and Christopher Corr:

978 1 84939 312 6

'One of the best new
picture books of this year.'
THE TIMES